Operation Melody

Denise Ortman Pomeraning

Illustrated by Meredith Johnson

Augsburg
MINNEAPOLIS

To my granddaughter
Cori Knudten

OPERATION MELODY

Cover design: Hedstrom Blessing

ISBN 0-8066-2718-2   LCCN 94-72210

The paper in this publication meets the minimum requirements of American National Standard for Information Sciences—Permanence of Paper for Printed Library Materials, ANSI Z329.48-1984.   ∞ ™

Manufactured in the U.S.A.   AF 9-2718

98   97   96   95   94   1   2   3   4   5   6   7   8   9   10

Contents

Snow Plans

Melody White was pale and skinny. I didn't know her very well. That's because I mostly hung out with Byron Woodstock and Werner Tavish. Boys like myself. I'm Kirby Casey.

One day Melody didn't show up in school. Ermalinda Larson told me Melody was sick. Ermalinda lives across the street from our house. Most of the time she's a big pain, so I didn't pay much attention to what she said. Anyway, I figured Melody would get better soon.

But Melody didn't get better. Her sickness was serious. She needed an operation. That wasn't the worst part. The operation was expensive. Even with insurance, her parents couldn't pay for it.

When I heard that, I began to think more about Melody White. She didn't laugh if a kid had spaghetti on his chin, or if he tripped over his own feet. But she did laugh at other kids' jokes, even when they weren't funny. Melody was one of the nicest girls in our school.

Everyone in our church liked Melody and her parents. Soon "Operation Melody" was under way to raise funds to help pay for the operation. The Men's League planned a pancake breakfast in the church basement. The Ladies' Guild held a Pie Fest. Our Sunday school class wanted to help, too. The next thing I knew, Miss Colman, our teacher, picked me to be in charge of the fund raiser.

Oh, no! I thought, *Why me?* I always get stuck holding the popcorn at the movies. Or taking care of my kid brothers at a picnic. Being in charge was not much fun.

I told my best friend Byron about it while we built a snow fort in my front yard.

"Hey, for a good cause you shouldn't mind giving up an hour or two of your time after school," Byron said.

He pulled his cowboy hat down over his ears. Ever since he went to his uncle's ranch, Byron has worn that dumb hat.

"That's easy for you to say," I told him. I threw a snowball for my dog Duster. He loves to chase after them.

"A fund raiser is no big deal," Byron said. "All you have to do is ask kids to earn money for it. Cori will give her baby-sitting money. Other kids will, too."

Cori is Byron's sister.

"What will you do?" I asked.

"Shovel snow. The pay is good."

"I could do that too," I said. I looked over at the house across the street. Byron did too.

He knew what I was thinking. "Ermalinda would never shovel snow," he said.

"She could sell those peanut peppermint cookies she bakes herself," I suggested.

"Sure. Ermalinda would love to go around from house to house, bragging about her cookies," Byron agreed. "Other kids like Amanda Dahl and Werner can shovel snow. There's tons of it all over town."

He made it sound so easy. That's the funny thing about Byron. And I always believe him.

In no time at all, he said, the Kirby/Byron fund-raising plan would raise more money than the Pie Fest and Pancake Breakfast put together. Melody would have the operation and be healthy again. My parents would say what a good job Kirby Casey did on "Operation Melody." And Byron and I could finish our fort.

No big deal. Easy as falling off a log.

It seemed like a good idea at the time.

I called up everybody in our class. Most of them were happy to shovel snow for Melody White. I guess being in charge wasn't so bad, after all.

Melt Down

Our fund-raising plans were shaping up just fine. Everything was set. Then there was a change in the weather.

It thawed. Our fort got soft, then sloppy. Soon there would be no snow left to shovel. Our fund-raising plans were melting away with the last patches of white stuff.

That's when Jennifer Beck thought of "Jump for Melody."

Ermalinda ran over to tell us about it as Byron and I were trying to save our fort with frost we scraped from the freezer in the basement.

"Here's how it works," Ermalinda said. "We'll hold a jump rope marathon. Everyone in our Sunday school class will ask people to pledge money. The more we jump, the more money we'll raise for Melody. Cori and Amanda and I think it's a great idea. So does Miss Colman."

"Cori will bring in mega-bucks. She's a super jumper," said Byron, smoothing the fort with a shovel.

"Your sister's not as super as Jennifer," Ermalinda said.

Byron couldn't argue with that. No one we knew was better at jumping rope than Jennifer Beck. So Byron said, "I can jump as good as you, Ermalinda."

Ermalinda's face got as red as her boots. "We'll see about that, Byron! We meet in the church basement next Saturday—'Jump for Melody Day.' "

What about me? I thought. *I'm in charge. Don't I have anything to say about it?* Out loud, I said, "What about selling cookies? Baby-sitting? Washing cars?"

"We voted on it," Ermalinda said. "Rope jumping won."

I tossed a fast snowball at Ermalinda as she walked away. Byron did the same.

We both missed. And before we had time to duck, Ermalinda threw one at us. It sent Byron's hat flying off his head.

We stared at each other in surprise. Then I said, "I have some rope in my room. Maybe we should go inside and practice a few jumps. I'm out of shape."

"Who needs practice?" Byron said, dusting snow from his hat. "I can jump her socks off."

Easy for you to say, Byron, I thought. My feet, nearly as big as my dad's, got tangled every time I turned the rope. I couldn't get past three jumps without falling flat on my face. As a fund-raiser, I would be the World's Biggest Flop.

I felt more sorry for myself than I did for Melody White. I did not look forward to Saturday.

The Face in the Window

The rest of the week was warm. Our fort dwindled down to a puddle. No more snowballs for Duster to fetch. No more after-school hikes in the frosty air. Just private practice and more practice with a jump rope in the cleared-off space in the backyard.

When Duster tried to jump with me, I shut him up in the garage. "Sorry, pal," I told him. "I have enough trouble without having your tail in the way."

Duster cried and scratched on the door to get out. I gritted my teeth and kept on jumping the best I could.

I was getting a little better. By the end of the week I jumped four times before I missed. Not great. But it was two jumps better than when I started.

Things were looking up. Mom and Dad gave me big pledges. They thought "Jump for Melody" was a wonderful idea. If only I could keep from tripping all over myself on Saturday.

At least I was sure the good jumpers, like Amanda and Cori and Jennifer—*especially* Jennifer, would take the fund over the top.

When I looked out the window before bedtime Friday it was snowing. *Too late,* I thought sadly. The great Kirby Casey shoveling plan was scrapped.

It was still snowing the next morning when I came down for breakfast. Dad looked up over his coffee and cereal. "Do your best today, Kirby," he said.

From the way Dad said it, I knew there was still a way to go before Melody's operation was a sure thing.

Even after a week's practice, I didn't feel confident as Byron and I started off for church together that afternoon. Duster wanted to come along, but I told him to stay home.

Werner Tavish caught up with us in the alley. "I don't know how long I'll last in this jump rope business," he said.

"I have a way with ropes from my cowboy days," Byron said. "I can jump all afternoon."

Werner gasped. "You mean without stopping or resting?"

I happened to know Byron's cowboy days were two weeks on a dude ranch. But I had other things on my mind. *Why do my feet always step on a moving rope instead of over it? What if I fall flat on my face? Everybody will laugh.*

"I'm going to give it all I've got," Byron said. "My sister will, too. Down to our last breaths, if we have to."

When we turned out of the alley at the corner of the block, we saw Duster

15

trailing us. He wanted to be with me everywhere I went. Dogs weren't allowed in church. I sent him home.

Byron, Werner, and I walked a couple more blocks, catching snowflakes on our tongues.

We passed by Melody's house on the way to church. Icicles hung from the roof over the front window where Melody sat looking out. Her eyes looked big and dark in her pale face as she tried to wave. It seemed as if her hand was too heavy to move very much. But her smile was the same as ever when we waved back.

It was hard to look at Melody stuck in the house while we walked along so free and easy. She wouldn't be jumping rope today with the rest of us. Maybe not any other day, either. Not unless she had that expensive operation.

Good jumpers or not, it was up to us. All three of us were quiet on the rest of the walk.

We didn't even notice that Duster was following us.

Kirby in Charge

"Look, Kirby, your dog is here," Byron said when we reached the church. Sure enough, there was Duster. He came up to me, nuzzling my mittens, happy to be with me again.

I was glad to see Duster, too, but I frowned at him. He hadn't minded when I told him to stay home.

"You can't come downstairs with me," I said. "It will be a long wait 'til I come out. Be a good dog and lie down here." I pointed to the mud hall that went from the parking lot to the church basement.

18

It's called a mud hall because so many muddy shoes walk through there.

Duster is always grateful for any small favor. He said thank you with his brown eyes. Then he curled up next to a pile of jump ropes near the door.

We stamped our boots, brushed snow from our clothes, and went through the smell of wet mittens. Then we came to the smacking sound of jump ropes hitting the floor.

I looked around the room. It was set up for the big event. Tumbling mats were placed at one end for rest breaks. There was a table at the other end. On it were big pitchers of strawberry punch, bowls of juicy orange sections, apples, raisins, and chocolate chip cookies.

Some folding chairs stood in the middle of the floor.

"Let's move those chairs," said Byron. "We'll have more space to jump."

We got busy.

I had just shoved the last chair out of the way when Jennifer came in.

She was frowning. Her red hair stuck out around her head like a warning light.

"I can't find my jump rope," she said. "I left it in the mud room yesterday."

Ermalinda came over and patted Jennifer's arm. "That's too bad," she said.

"There are extra ropes lying around," said Byron. "You can use another one."

"You're wrong, as usual," Ermalinda said. "Jennifer is a one-rope person."

She turned to Jennifer. "Let's go tell Miss Colman."

Across the room, Miss Colman was talking on the phone. When her call was finished, she came over toward me. Her forehead was wrinkled as she put her arm around my shoulders and drew me aside.

"Something has come up. I have to leave for a little while. I won't be gone long. You take care of things here until I get back. You're a responsible boy, Kirby. I trust you." She patted my hand.

What could I say?

Then Miss Colman climbed on a platform and blew a whistle. The rope swishing stopped. "By now you all have your pledges. Ask Kirby for your score card. Mark your card with the number of jumps between each rest period. At the end of our session, I'll add up the jumps for your totals. Rest when you are tired. Keep in mind that every jump brings Melody White nearer to good health. Give it your best, class."

We said a prayer for Melody White and the success of Operation Melody.

Then Miss Colman patted my hand again, said how responsible I was, and left me with her whistle and the score cards. I was in charge.

A Missing Jump Rope

I just stood there. For a minute, I felt important. I was a responsible person—Miss Colman had said so. But I felt scared, too, because I wasn't sure what responsible meant or what I was expected to do.

I took a deep breath, like before I jump into the pool at the deep end. I handed everyone a score card. Then I picked up my rope, asked Werner to turn on the boom box, and "Jump for Melody" began.

I jumped twice before I tripped. I tried again and tripped. Byron, Ermalinda, and most of the others were off to a good start. All except Jennifer—and me.

No matter how I huffed and puffed, I couldn't get any mileage out of that rope. I really tried.

But Jennifer didn't try. She just stood there.

When it was time for a rest break, I blew the whistle. Everyone stopped jumping. Some went over to the snack table. I went over to Jennifer.

"What's the matter?" I asked.

"No rope," she said. She pressed her lips together in a tight line.

"Want to use mine?" I asked hopefully.

Jennifer shook her head.

"What happened to it?"

"It disappeared."

"Have you looked everywhere?" I asked.

"Yep. It's gone."

Now was my time to be responsible. "I'll check it out," I said. I turned to the others. "Jennifer's jump rope is missing," I announced.

"We already know that," yelled Ermalinda.

Werner walked over to Jennifer and asked, "When did you last see your rope?"

Ever since he found his cousin's missing cat in the clothes dryer, Werner thinks he's a hot-shot detective.

"I had it after Bible study yesterday," Jennifer said.

Werner took a notebook out of his pocket and wrote something in it. "Where were you at that time?"

"Right here. I was practicing. I reached 387 jumps, my all-time record."

"And then what did you do?"

"I put it in the heap of ropes in the mud hall."

"And it's not there now?" Werner asked.

"Of course it's not there now," said Ermalinda. "Jennifer looked there very first thing. That rope just disappeared."

"Mysterious," mumbled Werner, scribbling in his book.

There was a buzzing murmur in the room. Jennifer was the best jumper in the class—in the whole world, maybe. Without Jennifer, "Jump for Melody" wouldn't work.

We hunted high and low for Jennifer's rope, beginning with the kitchen. I found a sack of apples there, but no rope. Werner searched behind the coat rack. All he found was a bunch of hangers that fell off the rack with a clatter.

Ermalinda went out to the mud hall to double-check and came back shivering. Luke and Amy Alt checked the rest rooms. Other kids looked beneath the tumbling mats and in every corner they could think of.

While we searched, Jennifer just stood there with her lips closed so tight it looked like she didn't have any.

And when we gave up looking for the rope, Jennifer said, "I told you so."

"Byron didn't look anywhere," whispered Werner as he turned on the music.

"That doesn't mean anything," I said.

The music blared out. Ropes began to turn. Jennifer acted like an elephant who'd lost its trunk. She sat down on the floor and stared around her.

"That girl won't move an inch," Byron said, jumping fast. "It's a good thing you've got a few faithful jumpers, Kirby."

Byron was talking about himself, I knew. But I had a sudden thought.

"Where's your sister Cori?" I asked.

Byron kept on jumping. His voice came out in little puffs. "Piano les-son," he gasped.

"Amanda Dahl's not here, either," I said. Amanda and Cori were good friends and good jumpers.

"They'll show up soon enough," said Byron, stopping for breath. "How many jumps you got on your score card?"

"Not many," I had to admit. But I decided my four jumps were better than none. Every jump counted. Especially since our three best jumpers were out.

Cori's piano lesson would end soon, I thought. Then she and Amanda would take over. While I waited, I jumped.

The afternoon dragged on. *What happened to Miss Colman?* I wondered. *She should have been back a long time ago.*

Amanda and Cori didn't show up either. Where were they?

I was starting to worry.

Out of Control

The room was hot and sweaty. The noise grew loud. Then louder. Kids on rest break crowded around the snack table.

"Hey, Kirby," called Luke. "There's not much punch left."

"Okay, I hear you," I called back. I sat down on the floor next to Jennifer.

"You're our best jumper, Jennifer," I said. "Won't you please try another rope?"

The other kids began to coax her, too.

"I'll let you read my new book if you'll jump," said Werner.

"You can wear my bracelet all day Sunday," said Amy, holding out her arm. "It's the one you like so much."

Peter held up a rope with gold handles. "You can use mine."

"No, thank you. I need my own rope to do my best."

Byron gulped some punch from a paper cup. "Take another rope and be second-best."

"No, it's no use. I'll never jump 387 times in a row again. Never."

"You don't need to jump 387 times. Just 57, or 27," said Ermalinda.

"Or even three or four," I said. "That's the most I can manage." I held up my score card to prove it.

Jennifer just sat there, shaking her red head.

Suddenly Byron lost his cool. He smashed the paper cup beneath his foot and gave it a kick. "Cut the act, Jennifer. Get out on the floor and jump!"

Ermalinda's face turned bright red, the way it always does when she is mad. She stepped in front of Jennifer. "Quit picking on my friend, Byron Woodstock!"

"Who's picking? It's not my fault she lost her old rope," answered Byron.

Jennifer jumped to her feet. "Don't say things about my rope. Last week you played cowboy with it. You said it was a neat lariat to round up horses and cattle."

"That was last week, and I gave it back to you, didn't I?" Byron said. "Buzz off!"

He grabbed his rope and began to jump on one foot, grinning like a pumpkin head. First his left foot, then his right.

"You're a show-off!" said Ermalinda. Then she jumped on one foot, too. That made Amy think of jumping backward. After that Ermalinda jumped backward on one foot. The next thing I knew, their ropes got tangled, and they bumped into Werner.

Crash! Werner landed on the floor. So did Ermalinda.

Things were out of control.

I hurried to the snack table. Things weren't much better there, either.

"Luke drank all the punch," said Amy, holding up an empty pitcher.

Luke made a face. "You ate all the oranges."

"There was only one. And Peter took the last cookie."

Peter was a first grader with an empty space between his front teeth. The corners of his mouth turned down. "My feet hurt. And I'm hungry."

"I'm hungry, too. When will Miss Colman come back?" asked Amy.

"Soon," I said. "I'll get more apples from the kitchen."

Werner followed me into the kitchen, where I found a box of strawberry drink mix and made some punch.

He set his notebook next to a big bottle of pancake syrup. "I've investigated everyone in our class, Kirby." He looked around the room, to make sure no one was listening. "There are two suspects in the jump rope case."

The punch was ready. I picked up the pitcher and reached for the apple sack.

"Ermalinda said she could jump better if she had Jennifer's rope. Remember when she said that?" Werner asked.

"You weren't there when she said it."

"Byron told me."

"That doesn't mean anything," I said.

"Ermalinda is a suspect in the case. And the other suspect is—"

Just then Peter came in. "Where are the apples?"

"Right here. We'll share," I said, handing him the sack.

Peter went into the room ahead of me. I saw him take one apple from the bag. He slipped it into his pocket.

Those apples were gone in no time. All except the one in Peter's pocket.

Werner sat on a mat, scribbling in his notebook. I turned on the boom box, blew the whistle and began to jump. At every jump, my feet came down like two chunks of concrete.

Amy and another girl stood in a corner, giggling. Peter sat on the floor and rubbed his feet.

"Jump for Melody" was going nowhere. And I was responsible.

"When will Cori be here?" I asked Byron.

"For the fourth time, I tell you I don't know."

"You don't have to be a pain about it," I said.

Ermalinda skipped rope in circles around me. She kept talking all the time: "Cori should be here to do her part. And Amanda, too. They should be ashamed, not showing up."

"Ermalinda's right," Amy said. "Fund raising is more important than piano lessons."

"More important than *anything*," said Ermalinda.

"Why don't you girls be quiet?" I yelled.

Ermalinda's face turned red. "Face it, Kirby," she said. "Jump for Melody" is turning into the biggest flop in the world. You better do something about it."

What could I do?

I went up to the mud room where I could think better. It was quiet and dark there. Too quiet.

I couldn't see Duster. He didn't come to greet me when I called his name.

I peered out the door. The parking lot was covered with snow! It came halfway up the door. And it was still falling, thick and fast.

My heart sank.

Miss Colman wouldn't be back soon. And I didn't want to think about Duster out in the snow. Duster was my best friend!

Where's Duster?

"Wow! We can build a new fort," said a voice behind me. It was Byron, looking at the snowstorm.

He jerked his thumb toward the basement. "It's a zoo down there. Everybody's squawking at everybody else. Ermalinda wants to know why Amanda and Cori aren't here. Peter's yelping about his feet."

"And now Duster is gone," I said.

"He got tired of waiting and went home."

"You're wrong, Byron. We closed that door after you came in here."

"Yes, and Duster came with us. You told him to lie down."

"If the door was closed, Duster couldn't get out."

"Someone who came in later left the door open. Or maybe Duster pushed it open himself."

"He could never make it home through that deep snow. His legs are too short."

Byron pushed his hat up from his forehead. He scratched his head, and then he said, "He made his getaway as soon as we left him alone. The snow wasn't so deep then."

"You don't understand, Byron. Duster wouldn't make a getaway—he wouldn't even try. I told him to wait for me. And that's what he would do—forever, if he had to."

"You told Duster not to follow you. But he did."

"That's different," I said. "He wants to be near me."

Just then Werner came looking for us.

"Something awful has happened. My dog is gone," I told him.

"Another mystery," Werner muttered.

I shook my finger in his face. "This is *worse* than a mystery. It's my pet. And he is missing."

Werner looked over the pile of ropes. He carefully looked over each one. Then he checked the mud hall for fingerprints. Next he checked for paw prints.

"Nothing much here," he said. "Mind if I take a look around outside?"

"It's all yours," said Byron, pointing toward the parking lot.

Werner pushed on the door. It didn't move much. He looked out, saw the snow, and closed the door. "I'll check in the basement. Maybe someone there saw your dog."

"The dog went home," insisted Byron. "I'll bet he took the missing jump rope with him."

"Duster would never do that," I cried.

Werner looked carefully at Byron. "Are you sure you didn't borrow that rope?"

"Quit nagging me, you snoop!" Byron gave Werner a push, knocking the notebook out of his hand.

"I'm trying to solve this case," Werner said in a scared voice.

When you are in charge, you don't want a fight on your hands. Quickly I said, "Let's go get something to eat."

"Eat" was the magic word. Byron, Werner, and I went back downstairs together. But things weren't much better there.

"Ermalinda made me miss," said Amy.

"You jumped too close," said Ermalinda.

Peter tugged at my sleeve. "I'm going to call my Mom. I want her to come and get me right now."

"How about some pizza? I'll order it," I said.

40

Peter's pout turned into a happy smile. Everyone clapped. They crowded around me at the phone, all talking at the same time.

"Order pepperoni," yelled Amy and Luke.

In one ear I heard Byron say, "Go easy on the cheese."

In the other ear I heard Ermalinda: "Lots of cheese, no olives."

"Don't forget the mushrooms. And green peppers," said the others.

"Wait a minute," I said. "Do we have enough money to pay for this?"

We reached into our pockets. We brought out nickels, dimes, and a few quarters. Byron counted it.

"There's enough money here for one pizza. No more," he said.

"Only one?" asked Peter in a small voice.

"Count it again, Byron. You made a mistake," said Ermalinda.

Everyone watched closely. Byron and Ermalinda counted the money together. Their answer was the same.

"One pizza is all we get," Byron said.

"That won't be near enough," said Peter.

I hoped I didn't look as disappointed as I felt. "One pizza will have to do," I said, picking up the phone.

There was no sound on the telephone line. I hung up and tried again.

"Here, let me try," Ermalinda said. She grabbed the phone from my hand.

Nine puzzled faces looked at me.

Ermalinda shook the receiver. She jiggled the switch up and down. Then she pointed at me and said, "Face it, Kirby. You are in big trouble. The line is dead."

Peanut Butter, Pickles, and Popcorn

Everyone was quiet. They stared at me. I was responsible.

Peter's mouth began to quiver. He was a first-grader. "I want to go home," he said.

"Don't be a baby," said Ermalinda. "Miss Colman will drive us home in her van."

I gave a little cough. "Miss Colman may not make it."

Ermalinda stamped her foot. "I definitely heard Miss Colman say she would be right back."

I tried to tell them—without making Ermalinda angry or making Peter cry—that Miss Colman could be stuck in the snow somewhere.

But I didn't explain it right. Everyone did get upset, even Byron.

"My sister is okay," he said. "My sister went straight home from her lesson before the snow got deep. She's home right this minute, gobbling up a good dessert."

In my heart I knew there was a difference between what Byron said and what he thought.

"You don't know for sure that Cori is at home, Byron," said Ermalinda. "I definitely heard her say she would be here after her lesson."

"She shouldn't have gone to the lesson," said Amy.

"Miss Colman, Amanda, and Cori, all missing. This is mysterious," mumbled Werner.

"And Duster," I reminded him.

"Forget Duster," said Ermalinda. "That dog's a pain."

"He is not," I said.

"Duster ate the cookies at my bake sale. I bet he ate Jennifer's rope as well. He knows he's in big trouble and he's hiding somewhere."

"My dog is not hiding," I said. "He may have been kidnapped."

"Huh!" said Ermalinda. "Who would want to kidnap him?"

I pretended not to hear her remark. To change the subject, I picked up my jump rope. "Don't forget what we're here for. 'Jump for Melody.' "

"I can't jump any more. I need nourishment," said Werner, flopping down on a mat.

"I don't want nourishment," said Peter. "I want food."

"Nourishment is food," Werner explained. "That's what the word means."

"Cut out your fancy words, Werner," said Byron.

"Let's see what we can find to eat," I said.

Everyone rushed to the kitchen, banging cupboard doors open and shut. One cupboard was so high none of us could reach it. "Get on my shoulders and see what's in it, Peter," I said.

I gave him a boost and soon he was teetering on my shoulders and peering inside. "Popcorn!" he said, waving a box.

Crash! He lost his balance and slid to the floor in a shower of fluffy white popcorn kernels.

While Peter gathered popcorn, Byron stuck his head in the refrigerator. "Our custodian must love pickled herring. There are three jars of it in here."

"Ugh," moaned Ermalinda and Amy together. "What else?"

Four English muffins. Part of a loaf of bread. Three thin slices of cheese. Peanut butter. Pickles. Ketchup. An almost-empty carton of milk. A big jar with a little jelly in it.

"There's a flashlight, too," said Byron.

"You're lying," said Ermalinda, going over to see for herself.

Byron reached in, took out a flashlight, and stuck it in front of her face.

"That's definitely a silly place to put it," said Ermalinda.

"I don't think so," said Werner. "I always keep a flashlight in the refrigerator. A cold battery will last longer."

Ermalinda didn't answer. She helped carry the food to a table—everything but the pickled herring.

We added everything we found in the cupboards: graham crackers, coffee, teas, more of the strawberry drink mix. And a big can of spaghetti.

Amy put out some knives and spoons. Ermalinda found a can opener and opened the spaghetti can. We each took a helping of cold spaghetti.

For the first time in history, Ermalinda didn't gripe. Even if she did, we wouldn't have listened. We were busy at the table, making our own meals.

I put popcorn and pickles over peanut butter on one slice of bread. Then I heaped on cold spaghetti and small hunks of cheese. I sprinkled that with ketchup, and placed a graham cracker on top, because there wasn't any more bread. I washed it all down with strawberry drink.

When we ran out of cheese and pickles and jelly, we dug into the peanut butter and ate it straight from the jar. Nobody wanted to try the herring.

After that, Luke remembered a candy cane he had in his back pack. It was left over from Christmas and very sticky. He broke it up and gave some to each of us. No one said anything about the dog hair on it.

And just about that time, Peter suddenly found the apple in his pocket. No one asked how it got there.

"Let's share it," he whispered, so I cut it into little pieces and Peter passed them around.

We sat around the kitchen eating, nice and friendly. Even Jennifer began to talk. "Our parents will worry when we don't come home."

"Mom thinks I'm with Miss Colman. She doesn't know we're alone," said Peter, gulping a big glob of peanut butter.

"We'll find a way to get home," I said. *But how?* I wondered.

Suddenly the room went dark.

Snow Cream

I blinked my eyes in the darkness. *What now?* I thought.

Peter grabbed my arm. The lights came on. Then off again. And on.

"Too much snow on the electric lines. We may be in for a power failure," said Werner.

Oh, no! I hurried to get the custodian's flashlight.

I set it down next to the bottle of syrup left over from the pancake breakfast.

The syrup made me think of a book I read. Some children mixed syrup with clean snow and ate it. They called it snow cream. I told the group about it.

"Neat idea," said Byron, putting on his hat. "Let's go for it."

Everyone jammed on boots and mittens and hurried to the door to the parking lot. Outside it looked like a Christmas scene in a plastic snow globe when you shake it up and down. Lamplights glimmered through the falling snowflakes. No traffic moved along the street. A parked car was almost buried in snow. And Duster was nowhere to be seen.

Byron and I grabbed shovels, taking turns with Luke and Ermalinda. We shoveled and shoveled, and cleared a space just outside the door. The snow piled high on each side of us. Higher than the walls of our fort.

At last it was time for snow cream. Byron and I stood in our cleared-off space. Most everyone waited in the hall, each with a spoon in hand. Amy handed us dishes through the open door. Ermalinda stood beside her. Werner waited behind Ermalinda, ready with the syrup.

Byron and I piled snow into the dishes, one by one, and handed them to Ermalinda. She passed each dish to Werner who poured on the syrup.

The snow cream went over big. Everyone asked for second helpings. Duster loves ice cream. I wished he were here to taste the snow cream.

We stood around in the mud hall and licked the syrup from the spoons.

It's not so bad, being in charge, I thought.

"Making snow cream is fun," said Luke.

"And eating it is more fun," said Peter. "I want more."

Peter went into the cleared space outside and said, "I'll get it myself." We watched through the open door. He held up his dish, laughing, trying to catch snowflakes in it.

Suddenly a wild wind began to blow. Whoosh! Byron grabbed his hat to keep it from flying. The dish spun out of Peter's hand. Falling snowflakes turned from big and soft to small and mean.

Another gust of wind. And Peter slipped and toppled over.

Byron and I helped Peter to his feet and into the hall. Just inside the door, I stopped to give one more call to my dog.

Wham! The wind slammed the door shut. We headed back downstairs. I was first. Peter, still puffing from his fall, came behind me.

The lights were on in the basement. It was empty, except for a girl with bright red hair whose back was turned to us. She was jumping rope.

I waved back to the others to be quiet.

Peter pushed in front of me so he could watch. "It's Jennifer," he whispered. "She's using my rope."

Jennifer's yellow sneakers lightly touched the floor, up and down, up and down—"fifteen, sixteen, seventeen," she counted in a sing-song voice, "eighteen, nineteen"—and then she stumbled.

The rope twisted around her ankles. She pulled it away, turned around, and saw us. "I can't," she said.

She slumped to the floor and put her head on her folded arms. Her shoulders shook.

Jennifer Beck was crying.

In the Dark

Jennifer sat on the floor, crying. I had never seen her cry before. I didn't know what to say or do.

If only Miss Colman would come back, I thought. Our teacher would know what to say.

But Miss Colman wasn't there. It was up to me.

"You jumped nineteen times without missing," I said. "I wish I could jump that well."

Jennifer looked up. "I'm not good enough. I can't reach 387," she said.

Not good enough! Jennifer was better than good. She was super-stupendous. Everyone knew it. But it's hard when everyone expects you to be good at something. And then you fail. Just like Miss Colman thought I was good at being responsible. And I wasn't.

Ermalinda shoved in between Jennifer and me. "I'm not trying to get a high score for *me*," Ermalinda said.

"That's right," said Luke. "We're doing it for Melody."

Then Byron said, "I'm so good, I've gone over my pledge already. From now on, Jennifer, whatever I jump, you can add to your score."

"You can use my score, too," said Peter. "My mom won't care. She'll give the pledge money just the same."

Then everyone in class spoke up: "You can have my score."

"And mine."

"Mine, too."

Jennifer coughed and wiped her eyes, and tried to look like she wasn't crying. She stood up.

And just then the electric power failed. The lights went off. Then on. I made sure my flashlight was nearby. We moved closer to one another.

"Add our scores together, will you, Werner? Before the power goes off again," I said.

I looked over his shoulder as he flipped his notebook pages. He turned from "Missing Rope Clues" to a new page and wrote, "Scores of All of Us Put Together."

Werner is a whiz at math. He collected our score cards and carefully looked them over. "All together we have a total of 4613 jumps."

I put the cards in the bowl that had been filled with juicy red apples. "From now on, we'll try for one total goal," I said.

I reached over and took Jennifer's hand. It was cold and shaking. Peter grabbed my other hand. His was warm and small.

Without saying a word, our class stood in a small circle, holding hands. Outside, the wind screamed and rattled the windows. We were shut off from our teacher, our pets, our parents, the world.

Werner turned on the music.

Slowly Jennifer picked up a rope. She swung it over her head in an arch. A cheer went up.

"Jump, jump, jump! For Melody White!"

Peter kicked off his shoes. "It's my shoes that hurt, not my feet," he said. "I can jump now."

Ropes began whacking the floor. We took turns keeping score for each other.

Byron did 102, 135, and 203 before he stopped to rest. His score for that period was 440.

After each rest, we did as many more jumps as we could in the flickering light.

At last the power went off for good. The music stopped. The ropes stopped turning. All but Jennifer's.

I beamed the flashlight on her. Standing in the dark, we watched Jennifer jump. Her feet hardly seemed to touch the floor. Her eyes were shining and her red hair bounced.

We began to chant with her, "Mel-o-dy seven, Mel-o-dy eight, Mel-o-dy nine." On and on to 350—380—389—and then 400, without missing a step.

We were shadows in the darkness, clapping for Melody—and for Jennifer, too.

I held the light for Werner as he added Jennifer's score to the "Scores" page.

"Look at this!" he shouted, almost knocking the light from my hand. "7501 total."

"Well," said Ermalinda. "This is not the flop I expected."

I gave a big sigh of relief.

And then Ermalinda said, "We didn't find the missing rope."

"I'm still working on the rope mystery," Werner said. "I found out something else."

"You did?" I asked.

"Yes, I found out Jennifer is not a one-rope person."

Jennifer laughed, and she grabbed another rope. I moved the light fast to keep up with her trick jumps—the crossover, and the tap toe, the wing ding, and the kick back.

When she stopped for breath, Byron said, "Shine that light on me, Kirby. It's my turn."

He tapped the floor in front of him with one heel while he skipped with the opposite foot. "That's called the heel-to-heel," he said. And took a deep bow.

Next my spotlight turned on Ermalinda and Amy. They jumped together with one rope.

And finally, when we didn't have another jump left in us, we plopped down to rest.

The wind stopped screeching. The window didn't rattle. Peter and Luke fell asleep with their heads on the same mat.

I wanted to tell Melody about our success. If only the phone would work.

The girls sat close together against the wall. Byron lay on the floor with his hat over his eyes. No one cried or yelled at anyone else.

But the room that had been so hot grew cold.

"No electric power, no heat," Werner said.

First we put on our jackets, then our caps, to keep from shivering.

Ermalinda tried the phone. It was still dead.

Do our parents know we are shivering here alone? I wondered. I had to find a way to let them know we needed help. A phone booth stood on the corner not far from our church. Was that phone working? If it was, could I get there in snow drifts as high as my waist?

We had a long night ahead of us in the cold, dark basement.

Ermalinda's loud voice came through the darkness. "It stopped snowing. Someone should go for help, Kirby."

"We might shovel our way to the phone," I said.

"Count me out," said Byron. "I'm beat from all my jumping. How many jumps did you rack up, Kirby?"

I knew what Byron was thinking. He thought that, no matter how I tried, I didn't jump as many times as most of the others. And that holding a flashlight wasn't a very responsible job.

"They'll come and get us sooner or later," he mumbled. And he settled down on his mat.

It was up to me again. Slowly I put on boots and mittens and started for the mud room. I handed him the flashlight. "Take good care of it. You may need it if I don't get back," I said.

Headlights in the Snow

"Wait a minute, Kirby," yelled Ermalinda. "I'm coming with you."

A few minutes later the two of us groped our way through the narrow mud room. It was a black hole. And twice as cold as the basement. I kept bumping into things. My foot tangled with a shovel. It hit the floor with a bang.

"Did you hear that noise?" I asked.

"Definitely. You knocked something over."

"No, not that. I mean *that* noise, outside."

A chugging sound, a grinding, shoving sound.

Ermalinda and I almost fell over each other in our hurry to get outside the mud hall. We pushed open the door, pell-mell into the snow.

Two round, bright headlights were coming toward us. It looked like some monster from outer space. We scrambled to our feet and backed up against the wall. The thing came closer. I blinked and turned away. Then I made myself look again.

"It's a snow plow," I yelled.

The plow was churning big chunks of snow up and around, making a path for the truck behind it. A strange man with a black mustache and a fur hat was driving the truck.

And beside him was a woman.

"Miss Colman!" I cried.

The truck and plow pulled up beside us. The doors opened and out tumbled Duster. He jumped all over me, barking and yelping. I hugged him as he wriggled with joy, licking the snow off my face and my mittens. And then came the driver and Cori and Amanda.

And Miss Colman, who threw her arms around me and kept asking, "Are you all right? Are you all right?"

Ermalinda put one hand on her hip. "We definitely thought you would be here before this," she said.

"Let's all get inside," said Miss Colman.

Miss Colman led the way with the help of the stranger's flashlight. I was last. Duster danced around my heels, all the way into the basement.

All the sleeping kids woke up. There was a lot of explaining and hugs and noise.

Miss Colman's glasses fogged up and she took them off to wipe them with her scarf. Then she introduced the mustached man who held his light so we could see his face.

"Mr. Panelli is a newspaper reporter," Miss Colman said.

The reporter grinned and propped his powerful flashlight on the table so that we could see each other.

"Look at Duster!" said Ermalinda. "He's wearing Jennifer's jump rope."

Everyone looked at Duster. A rope dangled from his collar. "How did he get that?" I asked.

"He got it from me," answered Cori. "I took the first rope I found. I left a note to tell you we needed it for a leash."

"We didn't find a note," I said.

"I'm sorry," Cori said. "I didn't know the rope belonged to Jennifer. Were you looking for it?"

"Definitely we looked for it," said Ermalinda.

"We wanted a leash to take Duster with us," said Amanda.

"Why? Where?" I asked.

"To Melody's," Cori explained. "She was lonely. Her friends were at church, jumping rope."

"We saw her looking out the window, and thought we should visit her," Amanda said.

"Melody doesn't have a pet. And when we saw Duster waiting here, we thought he would cheer up Melody." Cori patted Duster's head.

"And he did," said Amanda. "We brought him to Melody's house and he did tricks and made her laugh out loud."

Duster's tail thumped on the floor when he heard his name.

"Melody hasn't laughed in a long time," said Miss Colman. "Cori and Amanda were excused from their piano lesson and came here to tell me their plan."

"Our plan was to leave Duster there with Melody, then come back to the gym and jump," said Cori.

"But we couldn't get back because of the snowstorm," added Amanda.

"And Mr. Panelli was there," said Cori as she took the rope from Duster's collar.

I looked over at the reporter. He was bent over near the light, taking notes.

"When Mr. Panelli heard about Operation Melody, he went to her house to learn more about it," said Miss Colman.

"But Miss Colman, why did you leave us?" asked Peter in a sleepy voice.

Miss Colman wiped her glasses again. "I received a phone call from Mrs. White, Melody's mother. She told me about a storm warning she heard on TV."

"Mrs. White didn't want us to go out in the storm," said Cori, handing the jump rope to Jennifer.

"So I left here in my van to get the girls," Miss Colman said. "I told Kirby I would be right back. But the van got stuck. We wouldn't be here yet if it had not been for the kindness of Mr. Panelli. He is writing a story about Melody for his newspaper."

"And what a story!" said Mr. Panelli. "A bunch of kids go all out to help a sick child. And they end up marooned half the night in a snowstorm."

"We definitely went over our pledge promises, Mr. Panelli. Be sure to put that in your story," said Ermalinda.

"I can provide you with the numbers," Werner said, showing his notebook.

"Sounds like Operation Melody was a real success," said the reporter.

"It was a joint effort," said Werner. "That means we did it together."

"And Kirby Casey was in charge," said Miss Colman.

Mr. Panelli grinned and picked up his flashlight. "What do you say we make a joint effort to get out of here?"

With Mr. Panelli's help, we all got home safely. The next day, I read his story in the paper.

Many other people read it, too. In a short time, it seemed like everyone in town made pledges to "Jump for Melody."

Enough money was raised to pay for the operation. Melody isn't pale and skinny any more. She's back in school and church. Miss Colman said Melody will be jumping rope with the rest of us next year.

And maybe, with practice, I'll even do a few trick jumps myself, like the heel-to-heel or the tap toe.